M

THE MISTAKES THAT MADE US

Confessions from Twenty Poets

selected by
IRENE LATHAM and CHARLES WATERS
illustrated by MERCÈ LÓPEZ

Carolrhoda Books
Minneapolis

CONTENTS

INTRODUCTION

Out of difficulties grow miracles.

—Jean de La Bruyère

Mistakes.

We all make them. Some mistakes happen by accident, while others are deliberate. Some mistakes we regret, and others we laugh about. Even the most innocent mistakes can leave us feeling frustrated: *Why can't I do this right? I'm doing the best I can!* There are probably as many ways to make mistakes as there are people on the planet! And still, we often don't like to admit our mistakes, preferring instead to focus on our triumphs.

What might happen if instead of hiding, we were willing to talk about our blunders and misjudgments? The two of us have learned through our own friendship how connected we are by mistakes. How often have we said to each other, "That's happened to me too!" Or "That reminds me of the time I . . ."

Sharing mistakes is an act of courage and vulnerability.

Together, we learn.

We invite you to experience through poetry the real-life mistakes from some people who are brave and open and growing—just like you.

Irene & Charles

OOPSIE-DAISY!

Failure is the key to success; each mistake teaches us something.

—Morihei Ueshiba

It's one thing to make a mistake when it's you and you alone.

But when other people witness a mistake? That adds a whole new level of embarrassment! Public mistakes are hard to forget, but they can also give us some pretty great stories to tell.

These kinds of mistakes happen to all of us as we grow and learn. The important thing is to not let mistakes define you, and to keep moving forward.

MOST VALUABLE PLAYER

BY ALLAN WOLF

At the big soccer game,
as the whole world watched,
on a Saturday afternoon,
during the big tournament,
amid screams and gasps,
beneath stares of disbelief,
with heart pounding and cleats flashing,
down the green pitch,
over the halfway line,
around fullbacks and strikers,
between stoppers and wingers,
by dribbling, feinting, and then kicking
past the goalie frozen in awe,
toward the open net,
into . . .
the wrong goal?

Oh, I was proud as I could be.
It seemed like just a dream,
that day I was the MVP . . .
for the opposing team!

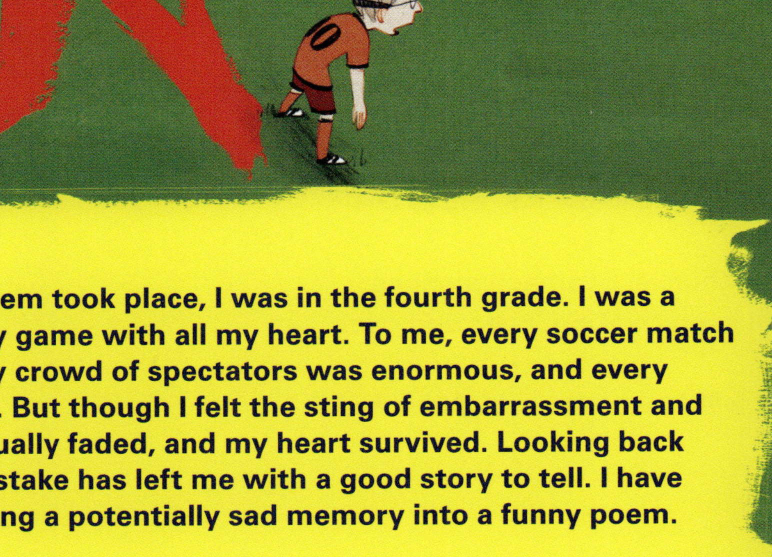

When the soccer match in this poem took place, I was in the fourth grade. I was a ten-year-old kid who played every game with all my heart. To me, every soccer match was a championship match, every crowd of spectators was enormous, and every minor "oops" was a major failure. But though I felt the sting of embarrassment and disappointment, that sting eventually faded, and my heart survived. Looking back from where I am now, my bad mistake has left me with a good story to tell. I have officially forgiven myself, by turning a potentially sad memory into a funny poem.

MATTER I ALLS

BY LINDA SUE PARK

There's an old saying, 'Pride goeth before a fall,'
which always made me picture a girl
all snooty and lah-di-dah, who trips and tumbles

into a big ol' hole because her nose was in the air,
and she didn't look where she was going.
I thought I knew what the saying meant,

but I didn't. Not really. Not until . . .

A slide show: "Mining Our Natural Resources."
Mrs. Fons tells me to read the captions aloud

because I am the best reader in the class.
Everybody knows it. (Especially me.
Sometimes Andrew gets picked. Second best.)

I read smoothly, my voice steady and clear.
I'm thinking that I should consider becoming
a news anchor, because I am really good at this.

Then I see a word I don't know.
I don't stop or ask for help—
I keep going, like a news anchor would:

"Engineers use different Matter-I-Alls—"

"MATERIALS!" Andrew yells.
"NOT MATTER-I-ALLS!"

The whole class spews laughter.
"She thinks it's Matter-I-Alls!"
"Doesn't she know it's 'materials'?"

Heart thunks. Stomach sloshes.
And I keep thinking, over and over,

How will I ever get out of this hole?

Second grade, Blackhawk Elementary School. Mrs. Fons and Andrew are real people. When this happened, I learned two important things. First, I began the (lifelong) attempt to stop comparing myself to other people. It's more important to compete with myself to do the best I can, no matter what someone else's "best" is. The second thing: I learned how to read the word "materials."

SCIENCE LESSON

BY DAVID ELLIOTT

The assignment? *Keep a journal.*
Eight weeks. Record all the trees,
birds, insects, and flowers
you find in your neighborhood.
Trees? Insects? Birds? Flowers?
Eight weeks? No way!
I'd do it in four hours.

One week passed. Two. Then eight.
My journal was blank.
But it wasn't too late:
The day before the homework was due,
I begged my friend Paula,
"Won't *you* let me copy *yours*?"

That night, I got busy.
Every insect, every flower, every bird, every tree
my friend Paula had seen.
I was on automatic. I was a copy machine.
Every insect. Every tree. Every bird. Every flower.
Page after page. Hour after hour.
Every tree. Every insect. Every flower. Every bird.
Entry for entry. Word for word,

including,
when I got tired at the end,
the name of my trusting but
misguided friend at the top of every page.
Paula Greene. Paula Greene. Paula Greene.

The mistake, of course, wasn't that I copied Paula's name. That was just stupidity. The real mistake was that I involved my friend in my own lack of responsibility. We both failed general science that year. Whenever I think of my seventh-grade self, I always think about this incident. Learning to own our mistakes is one of the most difficult parts of growing up.

EATING CONCRETE

BY MATT FORREST ESENWINE

It was only a curb,
not that high, not that big, certainly
not intimidating. I could jump it, easy.
Been biking since I was knee-high
to nothing
and I had to get to the sidewalk fast—
I'll jump it, that's what I'll do.

Probably didn't even get an inch in the air,

I went OTB,

Over.
The.
Bars.

Front tire slammed into that concrete
with me right behind, blowing off my pedals
feeling my bike twist over me, around me—

and me on the ground, stunned,
liquid iron on my tongue,
trying to hide a face full of stone, rubber,
and embarrassment with a capital *EM.*

Mad at myself, knowing
what I should have done, could have
done. Didn't do.

But now I sure do.

I was twelve years old and had barely started seventh grade when I was riding my ten-speed bicycle—not a motocross, not a mountain bike, just a normal ten-speed—and I thought I'd jump the curb. I learned the hard way that you need to practice these things before you can actually succeed at them. In reality, not many folks probably saw what happened, but it sure felt like the whole world was watching when it did. Never stopped me from biking, though. Do it all the time!

THE WANDERER

BY LACRESHA BERRY

"Lacresha Denise Berry!"
My mom stormed
through the neighbor's door
with furrowed brows
and worry in her throat.
Whenever she said
my entire name,
I knew I was in big trouble.
Earlier that morning
with our palms intertwined,
she looked me in my eye
and said, "Wait for your brothers
after school. No wandering off."

At the end of the day,
my first-grade heart
beat like a djembe
as I searched
for my older brothers.

Where were they?
Anxiety tickled my belly to my toes.

Was I in the right spot,
where Mom told me to wait?
Time escaped my six-year-old brain,
and I just couldn't wait any longer.
My feet wandered away from school,
to my little neighbor Jermaine's house
filled with video games
and peanut butter and jellies.
I forgot all about my brothers until I heard . . .
"Lacresha Denise Berry!"

Her voice let me know
it would be a long walk back home.

When we could no longer afford a babysitter to pick us up from school, my mother worried for my safety. She practiced the after-school routine with me every day. But on this day, when I didn't see my brothers, I forgot the plan and wandered off. I thought I did the right thing by going home with a neighbor, but when I didn't show up with my brothers, my mom got worried and looked all over the apartment complex looking for me. Talk about big trouble! Trust me, I never let that happen again.

STUFF HAPPENS

Mistakes are the portals of discovery.

—James Joyce

Sometimes we do things that hurt ourselves more than anyone else.

There are times when we let pride get in the way of common sense or when we cave to peer pressure. Times when we ignore that little voice saying, "Are you sure this is a good idea?"

These kinds of mistakes can offer us deeper insight into who we are and what really matters to us. They can provide guidance for how to treat ourselves with more respect and compassion in the future.

DARE

BY GEORGE ELLA LYON

Recess, third grade, on the sidewalk
by the concrete steps that led to the basement.
"I dare you to jump," Darlene said.
"I double dare you!" Jan said.
"Double-dog dare you!" Betty Lou put in
and Rita added, "I'll give you my candy money."
That did it. I got inside the railing put there
to keep anybody from accidentally doing what I
was about to do on purpose and
J
U
M
P
E
D
!
The jolt when my feet hit the concrete floor
shook my insides, scalded my feet, shocked
my bones. I couldn't run triumphantly up
the steps but had to stand still till everything
settled. "Are you OK?" Jan called down.
"Sure," I said, then climbed the steps slowly.
I took Rita's quarter—that was a lot! By then
It was too late for candy. Mrs. Unthank was ringing
the end-of-recess bell and anyway I couldn't
have swallowed water. I was a brave girl, though.
Everybody said so.

Fame from that stairwell jump faded fast. Decades later, something in my back went *sprong!* followed by pain so bad I couldn't walk. The ER doctor asked if I'd ever had a jolt to my spine. "No," I said. Later my physical therapist asked the same thing. "I did jump down a concrete stairwell once," I told her. "Well, there you go," she said. It was a long way down, but I had finally landed. Now I know that bodies remember. I wish I'd been more careful with mine.

YOU WANTED TO PITCH

BY JAIME ADOFF

Six o'clock church bells ring
I can smell hot dogs and sweet creme soda
Pop
Is in the stands
He is always in the stands
My biggest fan
Coach Frankie is running down the lineup
My mind is far away
I can almost taste the glory
YOU WILL see ME on SportsCenter tonight if SportsCenter had existed
Back then on that breezy early summer's eve
Circa late nineteen seventies
(Ah, but it was only seventy-eight—SportsCenter would have to wait another year.)
"Adoff's on the mound
Crome's behind the plate." My best friend since BEFORE the first grade
I take my slow superstar strut to the mound
Pound my glove like Guidry
All eyes on me
Pop smiles . . .
I had begged and begged
"Please let me pitch, Frankie, You've got to let me pitch."
"You're so good at second base/That's where you need to stay."
"Pleeeeeeeease let me pitch. Pleeeeeease!"
Finally, he said yes
With a wide grin
Devilish, perhaps.
They say when you're in a car crash
It's s   l   o w motion as the glass shatters into your face.
It was a bloodbath—my pitches barely hit the plate

Walk
Walk
Hit him in the leg
Hit him in the back
I stare at Frankie
Daggers from the mound
He looks down
Then finally mouths these four words
You wanted to pitch
There is no one to save me
but
myself.

My mistake was twofold. 1. I vastly overestimated my ability to pitch, and 2. As an eleven-year old in the fifth grade, I did not fully realize that all actions have consequences. This experience hurt my self-image in the short run, but in the long run, it taught me to dig deeper into my strengths and self-evaluate before putting myself in another precarious position. By the way, Frankie kept me in until I finally got myself out of the inning. I believe I let in at least six runs if not more!

SCISSORS

BY MARGARITA ENGLE

I was proud of my long, black braids
until I was eleven, when a girl at school told me
I looked too old-fashioned,
too foreign.

"You should cut your hair," she said, and because
I wanted to be her friend, I chopped off las trenzas
and became
a stranger.

I gazed at a mirror.
Where was I?
Who was this person
looking back at me, without a rope bridge
of braids to connect her to the women and girls
of my mother's homeland?

Cutting my hair was a mistake because I yielded to peer pressure. The pushy girl became my friend, but I ended up feeling even more lonely than before. It was the first and last time I ever tried to meet the expectations of someone who did not understand anything about me. From that mistake, I learned to ignore the commands of bossy people. I became strong enough to value my true self and to think independently.

MY SECRET

BY VIKRAM MADAN

I lamented to the teacher, "Your handwriting is absurd!
I've been trying hard all morning, but I cannot read a word.
I must walk up to the blackboard. I must squint and peer and stare.
It's the only way to make sense of the words you've written there!"

"Are you sure you don't need glasses?" Yes, my teacher was concerned.
"NOT AT ALL!" I'd hide my secret, even though I truly yearned
To be able to see clearly and not struggle when I tried
To watch TV or view blackboards or just play with friends outside.

You see, I was always reading—nose in book all night and day.
And my folks were always warning me, "Don't strain your eyes!" they'd say.
So then when my eyesight weakened, I was overcome with fright
That I'd done this to myself and I'd be scolded day and night.

So . . .
I pretended I was peachy, that my eyesight was okay.
And the school year went by—blurry—as I bumbled through each day.
But then one day I was running, and I fully failed to sense
That the gap I aimed to run through held a newly strung-up fence!

I ran straight into some wires, toppled, tumbled on my head.
Got a gash that needed treating. "You'll be fine!" the doctor said.
Then he gestured to a corner, "Read the lowest line you see."
But the eye chart looked so fuzzy, I was stumped as stumped could be!

There was worry, there was flurry, and then eye exams were next.
Everyone was so relieved to learn I only needed specs.
And I wasn't in big trouble. All my fears had been in vain.
As for me? I was delighted—I could see the world again!

When I got my first pair of eyeglasses at the age of ten, I did not, as I feared, get into trouble for "having strained my eyes by reading too much." Instead, I learned that grown-ups, like my parents and my teachers, really cared for my well-being and that I would have saved myself much suffering if I'd only told them I was having a problem. From then on, I was always sure to tell them if I needed help without worrying they might get annoyed or angry.

SILENT

BY KIM ROGERS

Mom sewed
a beautiful blue bonnet and dress
blooming in daisies like a summer field—
pioneer clothes I wore to stake my claim
on third grade Land Run Day.
"Ready, set, go!" yelled the gym teacher.
A few classmates and I
raced across the playground prairie,
alongside a covered wagon
made out of a red Radio Flyer.
We hammered a stick into soil
near the swings,
spread out a feather-soft patchwork quilt,
ate our brown paper bag lunches
of peanut butter and jelly
on our new homestead.
Dress fabric scratched my skin like sandpaper,
a cold sweat trickled down my neck from a too-hot sun,
my stomach turned green-apple sour,
and I shoved my barely eaten lunch away.
Here I was a Native girl
celebrating the day her Wichita ancestors' land
was stolen.
"Where are the Indians?"
I should have asked, had I known
the truth about history.
"What happened to us?"
"Don't you see me?"
But my voice wasn't there.
Not yet.

The Oklahoma Land Run of 1889 led to the US government opening more Indian Territory, land belonging to Native Americans, to white settlers. After a bugle sounded, they ran to stake a claim. These were dark days for tribes. When my boys were in third grade, I wrote letters to their principal and teachers explaining why I was pulling them out of school on Land Run Day. We'd celebrate our Wichita culture instead. Thankfully, many schools in Oklahoma have banned these reenactments because they see the harm it causes Native children.

BLESSINGS IN DISGUISE

My life is full of mistakes. They're like pebbles that make a good road.

—Beatrice Wood

Has there ever been a time in your life when you looked back and were glad you made a mistake? Maybe when a mistake led to a new opportunity or a new understanding?

These kinds of mistakes offer an unexpected silver lining, making us feel like we just received a high five from the universe. Often our favorite mistakes to share with others are ones that leave us thinking, "Thank goodness that happened!"

MY FAVORITE MISTAKE

BY DOUGLAS FLORIAN

Once in a painting, I painted some blue.
It was a mistake,
but what could I do?
I painted over the blue with a green,
but left some blue there,
a bit in-between.
Then I added some pink.
Bright orange as well.
And a red that resembled
a rusty old bell.
All the colors were spinning
like the spokes of a wheel,
with a whirling and twirling
and dizzying feel.
There were letters
with words,
and some pieces of twine.
There were secrets of secrets.
But the secrets are mine.

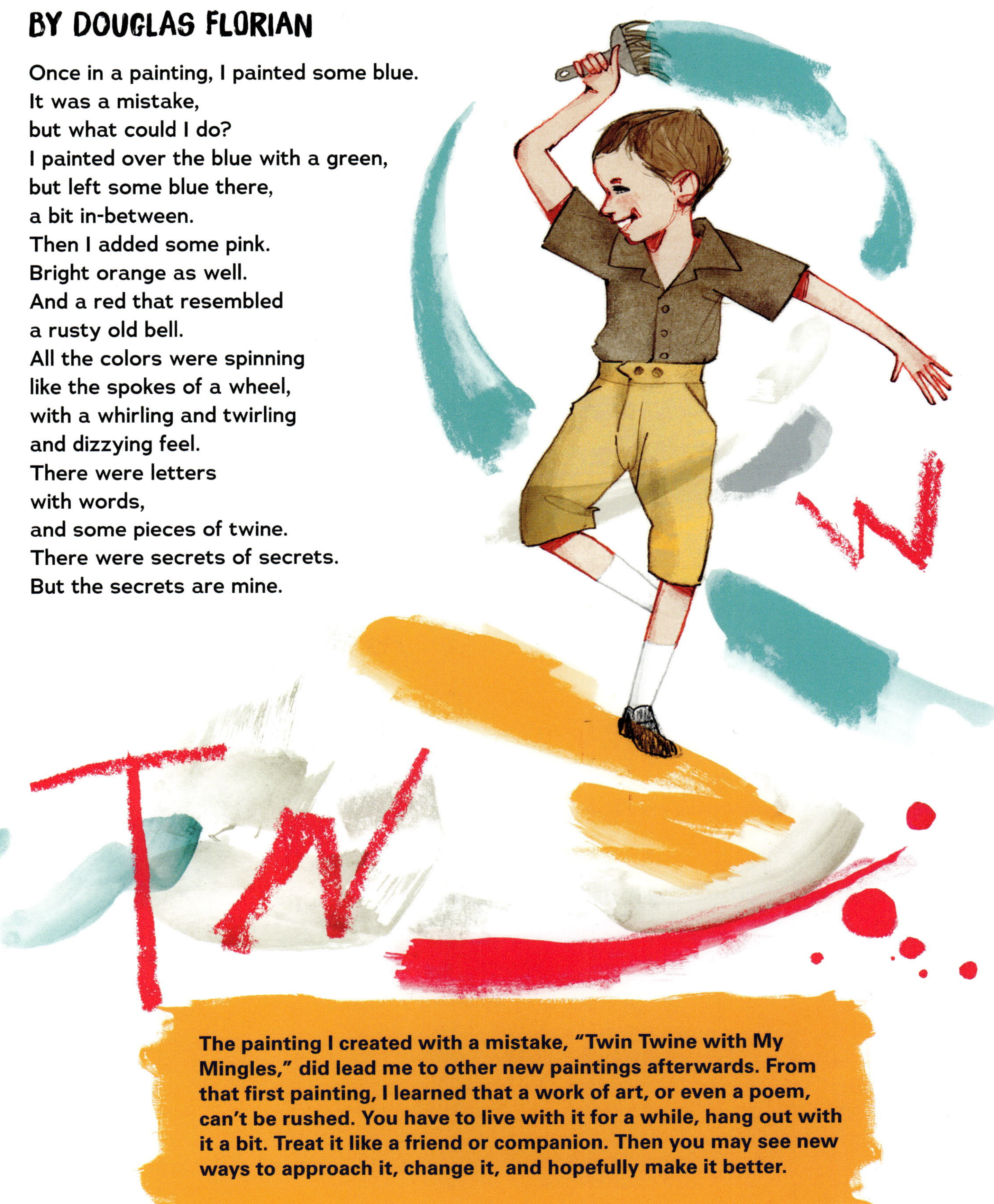

The painting I created with a mistake, "Twin Twine with My Mingles," did lead me to other new paintings afterwards. From that first painting, I learned that a work of art, or even a poem, can't be rushed. You have to live with it for a while, hang out with it a bit. Treat it like a friend or companion. Then you may see new ways to approach it, change it, and hopefully make it better.

WHEN I WAS MISS SPIDER

BY TABATHA YEATTS

I was at summer camp, doing my first play,
and I didn't understand rehearsing.
"Nobody can make you
do *anything*, James,
if you do not let them," I said,
looking at my script belatedly.

I thought, what's the point of
running through it over and over?
The only time what we do will *matter*
is when everybody is watching.

So I didn't try my hardest.
I said my lines late, and I sounded
like I was bored, which I was.
I laughed when I shouldn't.

Was the Narrator looking annoyed?
Did Mr. Grasshopper look concerned?
No one's watching! We're okay!

On performance day, I smiled
and wove a sprightly, springy web:
I paid attention, delivered my lines on time,
projected my voice so everyone could hear.

Although *I* knew I could do it,
my castmates were surprised—
I was funny!

Sometimes I've misunderstood a situation, like when I was twelve and I thought how well I acted in Roald Dahl's *James and the Giant Peach* only mattered if an audience was present. Not taking rehearsal seriously made my castmates nervous . . . they were certainly relieved when it turned out I wasn't actually a terrible actor. Acting with "oomph" was more fun than treating rehearsals like a chore. I realized this is true in many situations. Making an effort and doing things your own way can reap surprising rewards.

ESCAPANDO

BY JORGE ARGUETA

El día que nos escapamos
De la escuela con mi amigo Machuca
Nos saltamos el muro
Y riendo nos alejamos
Atrás dejamos los salones
Las burlas y golpes de los amigos
Y los maestros regañones.

Nos metimos los cuadernos
En medio de la cintura
Y bajamos la calle polvosa
Que conducía al río Acelguete.

Cruzamos el río
Saltando de piedra en piedra.
Más allá nos estaban esperando
Los altos y delgados árboles de guayaba.
Sin decir palabra
Machuca y yo subimos
Lo más rápido y los más alto que pudimos.

Enredados en lo alto comíamos guayabas
Como si fuéramos guaras o pericos
Cuando nos hartábamos las tirábamos al suelo.

Nada ni nadie podía tocarme
Yo era feliz volando y navegando,
Machuca igual que yo volaba
Y cantaba en lo más alto de los guayabos.

Cuando por fin cayó la noche y salieron las primeras estrellas
Nos bajamos y nos íbamos a nuestras casas.
Al día siguiente al ir a la escuela
Sonreíamos de guayaba.
Habíamos aprendido a volar a cantar a soñar.

Mi mamá siempre me decía, todos me decían, ve a la escuela, nunca faltes a la escuela, ese sería el mayor error de tu vida. Me dijeron, necesitas de la escuela para prepararte para el mundo, no cometas el error de no ir. Pero un día, cuando tenía catorce años, Machuca y yo saltamos el muro de la escuela y corrimos al río, al bosque, y nos subimos a los guayabos para jugar y sentirnos libres ¿Un error? No para mí. Estaba tan feliz ese día, y nunca me he arrepentido.

ESCAPING

BY JORGE ARGUETA, TRANSLATION BY ELIZABETH BELL

The day we escaped
From school, my friend Machuca
And I jumped the wall
And walked away laughing.
We left behind the halls
The classmates teasing and hitting us
And the teachers scolding.

We put our notebooks
In our waistbands
And we walked down the dusty street
That led to the Acelguete River.

We crossed the river
Jumping from stone to stone.
On the other side they were waiting for us
The tall, spindly guava trees.
Without a word
Machuca and I climbed up
As fast and as high as we could.

Tangled in the heights, we ate guavas
As if we were guaras or parakeets.
When we were full, we threw them on the ground.

Nothing and no one could touch me
I was happy flying and sailing,
Machuca was flying just like me
And singing in the tip-top of the guava trees.

When night finally fell and the first stars came out
We climbed down and went home.
The next day at school
We smiled guava.
We had learned to fly, to sing, to dream.

My mama always said, everyone said, *go to school, don't ever miss school, that would be the biggest mistake of your life.* They said you need school to prepare you for the world, *don't make that mistake.* But one day, when I was fourteen years old, Machuca and I jumped the school wall and ran to the river and the forest, and climbed up the guava trees to play. A mistake? Not to me. I was so happy that day, and I've never regretted it.

SKIPPING

BY JANE YOLEN

I was Little Red Riding Hood
who did not know whether or not
to follow the wolf.
So I shrugged,
turned my back,
and skipped off to Grandma's.

I was Cinderella
who found dancing in glass slippers
too close to dancing on knives,
so I skipped home barefooted
with a slice of cake for my little brother.

I was too smart and too smart-alecky
for first grade and other first graders.
I was already reading at a sixth-grade level.
I skipped right into second grade,

a kind of fairy tale,
that left me with no friends
who understood the loneliness
of a younger child in a higher grade
who read ahead of them
but was behind in everything else.

I did not do that kind of skipping
very well at all.

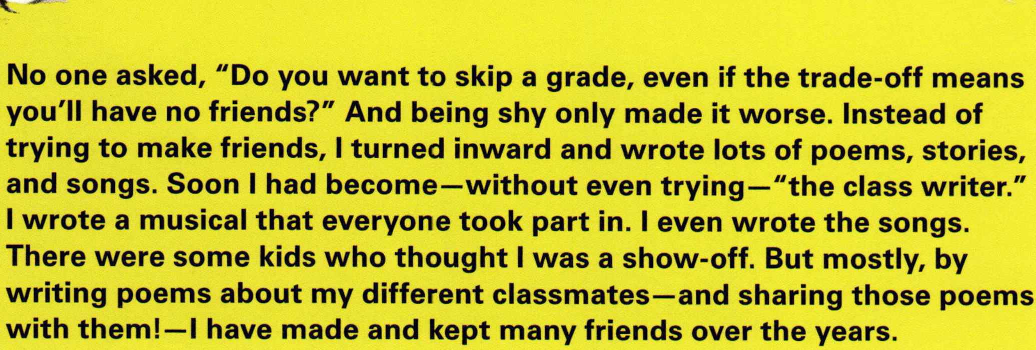

No one asked, "Do you want to skip a grade, even if the trade-off means you'll have no friends?" And being shy only made it worse. Instead of trying to make friends, I turned inward and wrote lots of poems, stories, and songs. Soon I had become—without even trying—"the class writer." I wrote a musical that everyone took part in. I even wrote the songs. There were some kids who thought I was a show-off. But mostly, by writing poems about my different classmates—and sharing those poems with them!—I have made and kept many friends over the years.

TOUGH LOSS

BY CHARLES WATERS

School bell rang, and waves of people headed
to their next class. I walked down the hallway,
found Mr. Hayes slouched against the stained,
chipped concrete wall, his eyes vacant
as a run-down parking lot.

He was the head football coach.
Knowing our team lost a squeaker
of a game on Friday, I walked up to him.
"Tough loss, Mr. Hayes." He grabbed my hand,
shook it hard, "Thanks, Charles." His eyes locked
into mine. His voice quaked. "Thanks so much."

At first, I was surprised he took the loss so seriously.
Until I heard someone whisper as I walked away,
"Poor Mr. Hayes. I can't believe he's at school
when his wife just died."
I felt like someone pulled a surprise onside kick
as I weaved in a daze to third period Spanish.

Of all the many mistakes I've made in my life, I've never been more thankful than I was for the one I made in junior high school. Back then—and even now—I've seen others tiptoe around a person when something tragic happens to them or their family. If I had known his wife had passed away, I never would have reached out to him and I wouldn't have known what to say. I'm grateful to have unknowingly provided comfort to a grieving man.

WHAT HAVE I DONE?

Mistakes are always forgivable, if one has the courage to admit them.

—Bruce Lee

The mistakes that most often make us hang our heads in shame are the ones that, intentionally or unintentionally, hurt other people.

Secrets, impulsive actions, inconsiderate words, or omissions—these things often happen so fast that our minds and bodies barely have time to realize what's happening. Then the moment passes, and there's no way to "fix it."

Mistakes like this often inspire deep regret and have the power to impact our thoughts and actions across a lifetime. Whether you are the one who has made the mistake or the one who has been hurt, it's important to remember forgiveness can be a great healer. When you forgive yourself and others, you claim your power and strength to move on to better decisions in the future.

PENCIL

BY NAOMI SHIHAB NYE

First day of first grade

John at pencil sharpener
sharpening ten pencils

We lined behind him
to sharpen one each

On his seventh
I poked him in the back
with my blunt nub

Isn't that enough?

He fell forward startled
slamming his nose
on the pencil sharpener

Blood gushed over
a pile of fresh paper
on our teacher's shelf
Sorry sorry sorry sorry sorry

I was herded to the coat closet
John scurried to the nurse

Teacher sent a note to my parents
This child carries the devil within her

Scary! My mother crying
through our whole dinner

I didn't know who he was

The pencil resting on my desk
saying all year
I'm still here

To be singled out as a "bad girl" on the very first day of first grade gave me certain alien status in my classroom. This probably helped me in the bigger life picture because I started writing little poems in the margins of my papers. After presenting one to my teacher as a "peace offering," she allowed me to pin it to the hallway bulletin board. An older girl read the poem, said, "I know what you mean," and my life as a poet began.

BIRTHDAY BREATHS

BY JANAY BROWN-WOOD

The light in my sister's face burned brighter than
the flames of the one-two-three-four-five-six candles
atop my birthday cake.

"Here," she said.
Eyes glowing. Shoulders dancing. Smile shining.
Birthday gift wrapped tight with a dazzling bow, presented
with outstretched arms and upturned palms.

I ripped the paper, pulled it piece by piece,
exposing each bit of the box until it revealed the gift inside.
A doll.
Another doll.
Another Skipper doll.
Barbie's little sister—from my big sister
to me.

"But I got this gift already! See? I don't want two!"
My booming voice bounced and rebounded
off the walls of a now-silent birthday party room.

"Oh," she said.
Her light dimmed.
Eyes darkening. Shoulders drooping. Smile fading.

My heart raced.
Remorse rising. Regret raging. Guilt overflowing.
Cheeks ablaze by red-hot shame as I watched her run from the room.

The light in my sister's face burned out like
the flames of the one-two-three-four-five-six candles
atop my birthday cake

blown out by bursts of my unbridled
breath.

After that, each time I played with my sister's gift, I tried to show her how much fun I was having. How much I actually loved my new Skipper, despite being gifted two on my birthday. Sometimes, my sister would even join in and play with me: Skipper A and Skipper B having a blast. Here's the best part: she forgave me. That was a hard-learned lesson, but one I still hold on to today. Though it may sound cliché, always remember: it truly is the thought that counts.

SHATTERED

BY IRENE LATHAM

Five little chickadees up against a wall—
two troublesome older brothers,
one sweet sister, one baby brother, and me.

Our parents flapping, firing questions:
Who did it? Why?
Confess now, or all will be punished.

My heart rattled behind hollow bones—
it was me—
but no peep dared leave the nest of my mouth.

Not with Papa eyeing my older brothers.
We know who it was.
Not with Mama pecking, pointing. *Admit it.*

As my brothers screeched their denials,
I settled into my feathers. No one suspected me;
of course it was my brothers.

We all went to bed without supper.
We all heard Mama cry.
I was the only one who knew why.

I'm not proud that I let my siblings be punished for something I did. At the time, when I was about eight years old, I was frightened and thought it best to keep quiet, to hide my mistake in order to maintain my role as the "good daughter." Now I know "good" doesn't mean "perfect," and a mistake is just a mistake; it doesn't make a person less valuable or less lovable. In fact, it's sharing our imperfections and being honest about who we are that opens the door to more loving relationships and more joyful living.

BETWEEN US: A POEM FOR TWO VOICES

BY APRIL HALPRIN WAYLAND

Hey, you—I kissed Charlie!

my BFF told me

But it's SECRET, so NEVER . . .

Oh, no *never*, I promised.

However.

I met a new friend. I thought, "I'll impress her."
I started to blather. Why would it matter?

This "friend" told another.

I still can't believe it—I promised I'd never. I promised *forever.*
HOW could I do that? I feel like a creep. How can I sleep?

Now I stare at your shoes. "I'm sorry. I shared your big secret."

You TOLD I kissed Charlie? And you say that you're SORRY?

I promised I'd never. I promised forever.

You PROMISED.

I promised.

I just can't believe it. You reassured me. I thought that you heard me.
But you . . . you betrayed me.

I stare at my shoes.

You can't even FACE me. I'll never believe you. We're over. We're through.

Nothing to say.
My friend walks away.

In middle school, my best friend since kindergarten whispered, "Don't tell anyone this, but I kissed Charlie!" Her secret burned in my throat—I could barely breathe. I told someone. My friend found out. We were never friends again. I'd made a terrible mistake. At times, I still stumble (surprise—I'm human!). When I do, I ask for guidance from a trusted friend, then apologize to the person I harmed. Face it: it's hard to be honest—but what a relief it can be! I have become more honest . . . and I can breathe.

THE GLUE THAT BINDS US

BY DARREN SARDELLI

My mother used to tell me,
"Think before you do."
I wish I would have stopped and thought
before I used the glue.

I tiptoed to the bathroom
and spread it on the seat,
then waited rather patiently
to prank my Uncle Pete.

It took a half a minute
for Uncle Pete to rise.
He bolted to the bathroom,
then got a big surprise.

My uncle started shouting.
He banged the bathroom wall.
I thought it was hilarious—
until I heard him fall.

I felt a sense of terror.
My heart began to race.
A mix of sweat and teardrops
descended down my face.

My aunt used melted butter
to remove the broken seat.
From that day on, I haven't played
a prank on Uncle Pete.

Growing up, I was a very impulsive kid. I would act without thinking and deal with the consequences later. Many times, the repercussions were pretty severe. This experience, which happened when I was around nine or ten, helped me think about how my actions could affect other people, and it changed me for the better. Luckily, my uncle was a really good sport about having a toilet seat glued to his bottom. From that day on, every time we were around each other and one of us had to use the bathroom, the other would say, "Don't get stuck!"

1
SUPER GLUE
2
4
5
6
9
10
11

ABOUT THE POETS

JAIME ADOFF is an award-winning writer of various young adult novels and children's poetry collections. His books include *Names Will Never Hurt Me, The Song Shoots Out of My Mouth: A Celebration of Music, Jimi & Me*, and *The Death of Jayson Porter*. www.therealjaimeadoff.com

JORGE ARGUETA was born in El Salvador and immigrated to San Francisco, California, in 1980. A prize-winning poet and author of many bilingual children's books and poetry books, he was named the first Latino poet laureate of San Mateo County. www.jorgetetlargueta.weebly.com

LACRESHA BERRY is a poet, performer, educator, and playwright. Her latest one woman show, *Tubman*, has been performed all over the United States and in Europe. This is her first anthology, and she's looking forward to writing more cool poems and stories for young people. She lives with her little fur child, Minty, in New York City. www.berryandconyc.com

JANAY BROWN-WOOD, PhD, is an award-winning children's author, poet, educator, and scholar. JaNay loves to write, bake, teach, and spend time with her husband, Catrayel, and her daughter, Vivian. She has more than fifteen books now available or forthcoming. www.janaybrownwood.com

DAVID ELLIOTT is the award-winning author of more than thirty books for young people, including the *New York Times* bestselling picture book *And Here's to You!* and three critically acclaimed YA verse novels, *Bull*, *The Seventh Raven*, and *Voices: The Final Hours of Joan of Arc*. David lives in New Hampshire with his wife and their rescue Dandie Dinmont terrier, Quiggy. www.davidelliottbooks.com

MARGARITA ENGLE is the Cuban-American author of many verse novels, memoirs, and picture books, including *The Surrender Tree*, *Enchanted Air*, *Drum Dream Girl*, and *Dancing Hands*. She served as the national Young People's Poet Laureate from 2017 to 2019. www.margaritaengle.com

MATT FORREST ESENWINE is the author of *Flashlight Night*, which received a *Kirkus* starred review and was included in *Encyclopedia Britannica*'s list of "11 Children's Books That Inspire Imagination!" He has nearly a dozen books to his credit including *I Am Today*. www.MattForrest.com

DOUGLAS FLORIAN was born and now lives in New York City. He has written and illustrated more than fifty children's books, including twenty-four books of poetry, such as the award-winning *insectlopedia*, *zoo's who*, and his recent *Zoobilations!* He has read his poetry at Carnegie Hall, the Museum of Modern Art in New York City, and the White House. www.douglasflorian.com

IRENE LATHAM is an award-winning poet and novelist who writes for all ages. Her poetry titles include *This Poem Is a Nest*, a book of found poetry, and *The Museum on the Moon*, a Lee Bennett Hopkins Honor Award winner. Curating poetry anthologies with her poetic-forever-friend Charles Waters is her new favorite writing adventure. www.irenelatham.com

GEORGE ELLA LYON was named the Kentucky Poet Laureate from 2015 to 2016 and is the author of many books including *Voices of Justice: Poems about People Working for a Better World* and *Voices from the March on Washington* (cowritten with J. Patrick Lewis). www.georgeellalyon.com

VIKRAM MADAN creates fun art and funny books for kids, including the 2023 Theodor Seuss Geisel Honor Book *Owl and Penguin*; the award-winning poetry collections *A Hatful of Dragons*, *The Bubble Collector*, and *Lord of the Bubbles*; and the Bobo and Pup-Pup early readers. www.vikrammadan.com

NAOMI SHIHAB NYE was the national Young People's Poet Laureate from 2019 to 2022. Her most recent books are *Everything Comes Next* and *The Turtle of Michigan*. www.poetryfoundation.org/poets/naomi-shihab-nye

LINDA SUE PARK is the author of many books for young readers, including the 2002 Newbery Medal winner *A Single Shard* and the *New York Times* bestseller *A Long Walk to Water*. Her most recent title is *The One Thing You'd Save*, a collection of linked poems. www.lindasuepark.com

KIM ROGERS writes short stories, poems, and books for young readers. Her debut picture book, *Just Like Grandma*, was published in 2023. Kim is an enrolled member of Wichita and Affiliated Tribes and is a member of the National Native American Boarding School Healing Coalition. She lives with her family on her tribe's ancestral homelands in Oklahoma. www.kimrogerswriter.com

DARREN SARDELLI is an award-winning poet and author. His poems are featured in twenty-five children's books in the US and the UK, including *What If?* and *Galaxy Pizza and Meteor Pie*. Darren has a knack for getting students interested in poetry. He's been to more than nine hundred schools, where he brings poetry to life and empowers people in extraordinary ways. www.LaughAlotPoetry.com

CHARLES WATERS is a children's poet, actor, educator, and coauthor of various books including the award-winning *Can I Touch Your Hair? Poems of Race, Mistakes and Friendship*. This is his first time (but not the last) being a poetry anthologist with his pal, Irene Latham. www.charleswaterspoetry.com

APRIL HALPRIN WAYLAND is the author of award-winning picture books, poems, and a young adult novel. She writes a poem a day and sends it to her friend, author Bruce Balan, as he sails around the world. Find her on www.TeachingAuthors.com and www.AprilWayland.com.

ALLAN WOLF is the author of many picture books, poetry collections, and novels for young people. His written work combines his love of research, history, science, and poetry. Also a dynamic performance poet with nearly a thousand poems committed to memory, Allan believes in the power of poetry to educate, enlighten, and heal. www.allanwolf.com

TABATHA YEATTS is a poet, author, blogger, and the editor of the popular *Imperfect* and *Imperfect II* anthologies for middle schoolers. Tabatha has three adult children and lives in Maryland with her husband, their two dogs, and dozens of plants. www.tabatha-yeatts.com

JANE YOLEN is the author of more than four hundred books for children and adults. In addition to being the recipient of many prestigious book awards, Jane has received honorary doctorate degrees from six colleges and universities for her body of work. www.janeyolen.com

For Mama, Papa, Stan, Ken, Lynn & MicaJon, with love and apologies. —I.L.

For Michele Weisman of Meet the Writers, Inc. Meeting you was no mistake. —C.W.

To Jordi, Mariana, and Txarli, who taught me how to fall. —M.L.

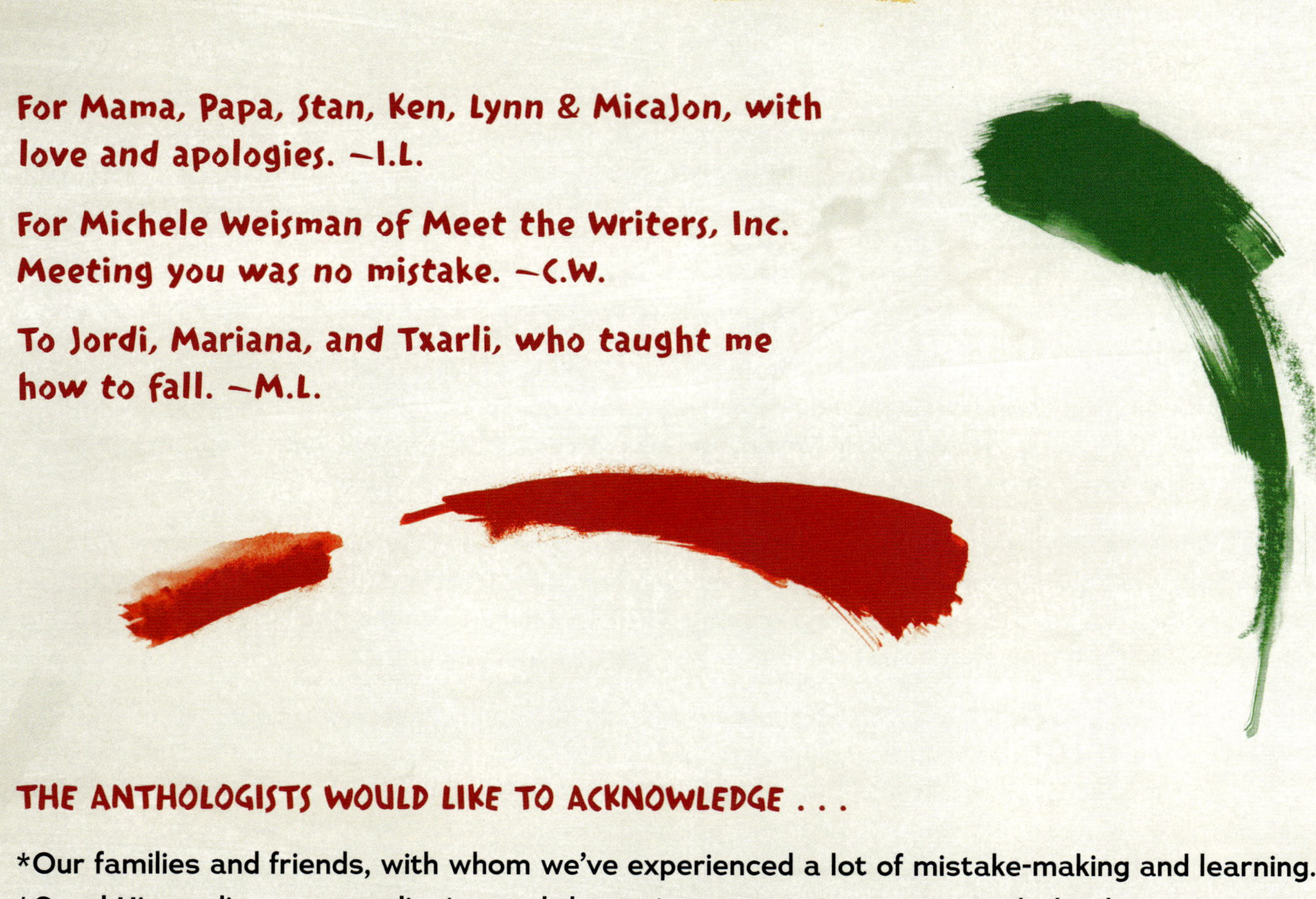

THE ANTHOLOGISTS WOULD LIKE TO ACKNOWLEDGE . . .

*Our families and friends, with whom we've experienced a lot of mistake-making and learning.
*Carol Hinz, editor extraordinaire, and the entire team at Lerner. #proudtobealerner
*Illustrator Mercè López.
*Traci Sorell, for assistance in the eleventh hour.
*The poets, for sharing their stories.
*And YOU, dear reader. May your mistakes make you strong and kind.

Carolrhoda Books®
An imprint of Lerner Publishing Group, Inc.
241 First Avenue North
Minneapolis, MN 55401 USA

For reading levels and more information, look up this title at www.lernerbooks.com.

Additional design element: Salman Timur/Shutterstock.

Designed by Kimberly Morales.
Main body text set in Adrianna Demibold.
Typeface provided by Chank.
The illustrations in this book were created with acrylic, graphite, ink, and digital art.

Library of Congress Cataloging-in-Publication Data

Names: Latham, Irene. | Waters, Charles, 1973– | López, Mercè, 1979– illustrator.
Title: The mistakes that made us : confessions from twenty poets / selected by Irene Latham and Charles Waters ; illustrated by Mercè López.
Description: Minneapolis : Carolrhoda Books, 2024. | Audience: Ages 7–11. | Audience: Grades 2–3. | Includes one poem in Spanish with English translation. | Summary: Twenty poets each share a poem about a mistake they made as a young person and also provide a short statement on what they learned from it.
Identifiers: LCCN 2023049170 (print) | LCCN 2023049171 (ebook) | ISBN 9781728492100 (library binding) | ISBN 9798765630242 (epub)
Subjects: LCSH: Errors—Juvenile poetry. | Children's poetry, American. | Autobiographical poetry, American. | American poetry—21st century. | CYAC: Errors—Poetry. | American poetry—Collections. | LCGFT: Autobiographical poetry.
Classification: LCC PS595.E77 M57 2024 (print) | LCC PS595.E77 (ebook) | DDC 811/.608—dc23/eng/20240206

LC record available at https://lccn.loc.gov/2023049170
LC ebook record available at https://lccn.loc.gov/2023049171

Manufactured in the United States of America
1-53147-51157-4/23/2024

NATURE
SUPER GLUE